Are You Sleeping?

Constanze von Kitzing

Barefoot Books
step inside a story

"Are you sleeping?" asked Little Lion.

Yes, the bunnies are asleep.

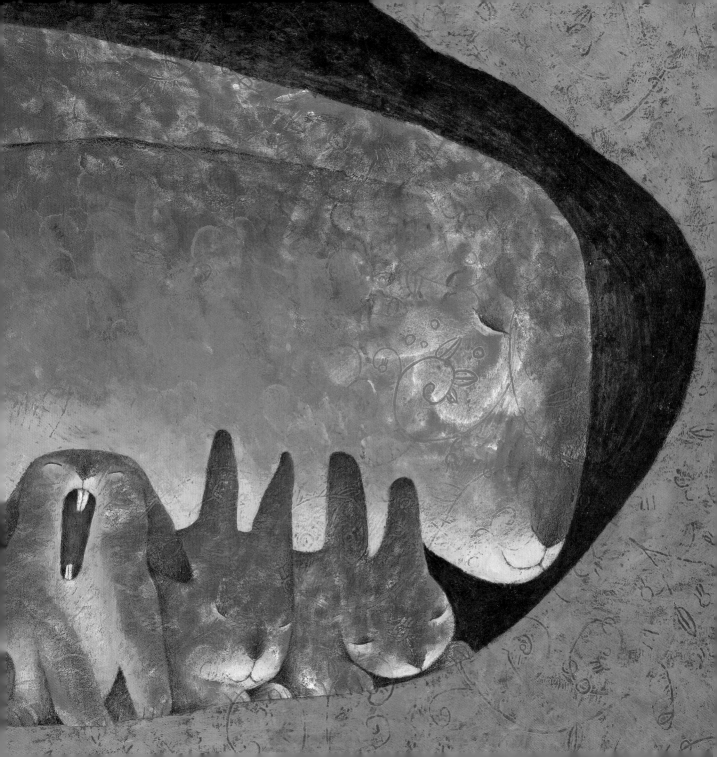

"Are you sleeping?" asked Little Lion.

Yes, the
giraffes
are asleep.

"Are you sleeping?"
asked Little Lion.

Yes, the elephants are asleep.

"Are you sleeping?" asked Little Lion.

Yes, the
birds are
asleep.

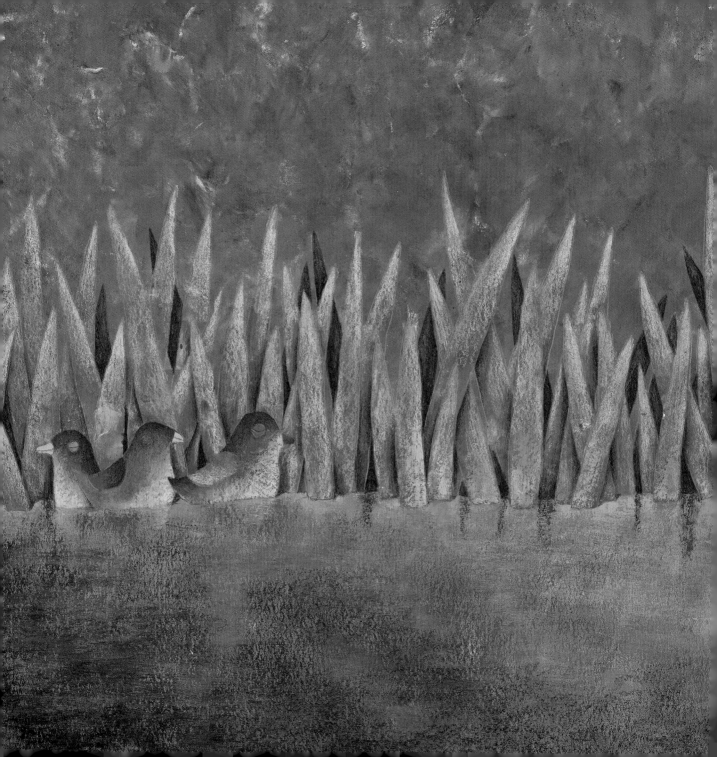

"Are you sleeping?" asked Little Lion.

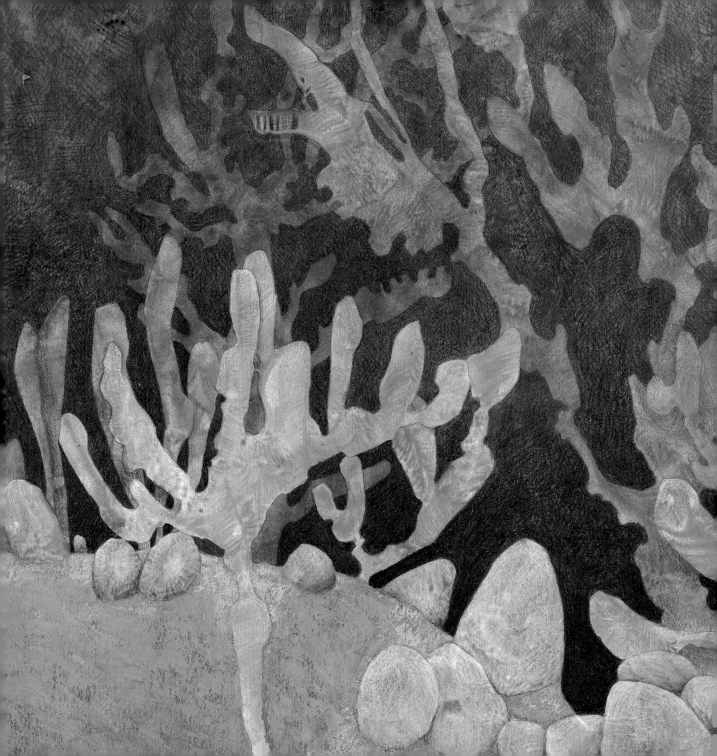

Yes, the seahorse is asleep.

"Are you sleeping?"
asked Little Lion.

"DO you want to play?"
asked the OWL.

"It's getting late . . ."
Said Little Lion.

"Are you sleeping?"
asked Mama Lion.

Shhhh . . .